Published by Ad Hoc Fiction.
www.AdHocFiction.com

Purchasing Information:
Paperback available from www.AdHocFiction.com
E-book available from all usual outlets.

Printed in the United Kingdom.
First printing 2019.

ISBN paperback 978-1-912095-97-1
ISBN e-book 978-1-912095-96-4

Homing

by

Johanna Robinson

AdHoc Fiction

To Gordon

I hope you enjoy the book and this little piece of history :)

love Johanna xx

July 19

For my parents, for everything

A Note on the History

While this is a work of fiction, and all characters – and their personal, individual experiences – are entirely fictional, the larger events did take place. The Norwegian teachers were sent to concentration camps; the paperclip was a symbol of resistance; men did escape to Shetland on fishing boats; and the tiny coastal village of Telavåg was razed to the ground, with the men and boys sent to Sachsenhausen and the women and children interned in a school. The village was also rebuilt after the war. The Norwegian resistance movement, countless courageous men and women, made a vital and unique contribution to the Allied war effort, in the face of incalculable risk and danger to themselves and their families. *Takk for alt.*

Contents

ENGLAND 1969

Pushing Atoms

I cleared most things out of my office yesterday. Today, I consider throwing my cards, a stack of farewells – addressed to Caroline, Carolina, Lina – into the already full bin, but I tuck them into my bag, next to the plain-framed photo of the twins when they were ten. They are sixteen now, and think they don't need me. I check my desk drawer; it's empty, apart from the crumbs of office life and the splintered, remnant scent of pencil shavings. I'm nostalgic before I've even left. From the corridor comes the compressed hum of a vacuum cleaner. 'To Lina. To the future!' my colleagues had toasted at lunchtime, as if I *was* the future. 'Come back and see us,' they said, and although I'd promised I would, as I close the blinds, I know I won't.

I pick up a handful of paperclips from the spill and tangle on my desk. There are families of them: big, thick-wired ones, impossible to corrupt into a bend, a statement more than a tool; and then there are the small ones, less than an inch long, thin and weightless.

These are the ones I've spent years fiddling with, on the phone, taking notes and messages: my memory charms. When I pull one apart, forcing each limb back on itself, it makes an 'S' of sorts. A broken figure-of-eight. Or a 5. A hook. These small steel ones are best for this habit: they unfurl more easily, forget what they were designed to be. They warm up, a feeble, fleeting heat, as I warp and twist them, the atoms pushing and jostling between my fingers. At the end of the day I'd sweep the clips across my desk and into the bin, like dead insects, a mesh of deformed prongs.

I gather my flowers in the crook of my arm and run my fingers across the ledge of the sash window, checking it's locked. The rain has seeped in and I wipe my hand on my coat. I can see my husband below, on the street, waiting for me in the car. I slip a paperclip into my pocket.

'Hello.' I push the bouquet into the footwell. 'They bought me flowers.' I lean over and kiss his cheek, which is patterned with the shadows of silver November rain.

The rain amplifies the silence in the car. 'Aren't you going to ask how my last day went?'

'Lina,' he says. 'It's your mum.'

In my pocket, in my palm, the paperclip is warming.

A Checklist of Belongings

A big, brown suitcase with leather handles. Stockings. A Norwegian passport. Our marriage certificate. Two ferry tickets to Newcastle. A bracelet, kept safe in a snagging swatch of lace. A photograph of my parents on their porch, my mother's hand blurred, as though she might be about to wave. My grandmother's earrings, inherited. My *bunad*: the heavy dress, sewn by the women, my mother, my aunts. A map, with our village clearly marked on it. A love letter from the boy I almost married. Lipstick. Cigarettes. My wedding skirt and jacket, and instructions from my mother on how to dye them. Two wedding photographs (one with my eyes closed): me and Arne, surprised and happy, standing on the church steps. A book of Norwegian poetry: his wedding gift to me. My brother's watch, his letters, all the things he collected. A scarf knitted by my oldest friend, whose wool would always smell of home. A thick English dictionary. A thinner Norwegian one. A Norwegian coin from this year: 1948. An umbrella.

A small weekend bag. A ferry ticket. A sick bag. A handkerchief. Ginger biscuits. A bus ticket. Maternity dresses. A gift for my father: a dead English butterfly, on a pin, in a box. A gift for my mother: pressed English flowers. Novelties for my already fading friends; I might have called them souvenirs if I hadn't been returning to England: *revenirs*, perhaps. A photograph of our house in the English countryside. Boots so high the snow can't get in. Three English coins, to show everyone back home; they have no holes in the centre.

The small weekend bag. Two English coins. Damp boots. Damp socks. Maternity dresses. A bus ticket. A handkerchief. A ferry ticket. Dried fish and brown cheese – for Arne, though I will eat it too. A list of names in my mother's handwriting: boys and girls, as though I may be in danger of forgetting.

My children's suitcases: a boy's, a girl's. My husband's suitcase. My suitcase. Four return aeroplane tickets. Luggage tags: outward/inward. Snacks for the taxi. Four British passports. A black dress. A black hat. Black gloves. Black tights. My grandmother's earrings, inherited. A fuzzy photograph of my mother, the only time she came to visit us, sitting under our pear tree. A piece of paper, my handwriting hidden in its folds, full of words I'd forgotten, or double-checked, for spelling, for sound. *Eulogy* in English. In Norwegian, *lovtale*.

NORWAY 1933

Strawberries

I am six and keen to please. My mother is on the back steps, hulling strawberries, and I am sitting between her knees, leaning against her thighs.

I pick up a strawberry. 'Your fingers are too small for this job, Caroline, I think,' she says.

I press my thumb below a stem, but all I make is a hole.

I pinch the skin on her arm and watch it sink and settle back where it belongs. It's not enough, so I push in with my nails until she makes a noise, as though it was just an accident. Curved little white lines dent her skin; around them, pink-juice fingerprints. Later, she whips cream, and serves the berries in five bowls.

Norway 1939

Bearskin

It has taken many years for Bjørn to become bear. When I was seven or so, there were only a couple of inches between us, although he was twelve. He was thin, but he was fast, his knees like huge ball bearings, and he would chase me through our house – through the front door, out through the back, across the garden to our grandparents' house, pretending to bite my ankles as we rose, clattering, into their hall, lured and howling like wolves, calmed by waffles and jam. Eventually he stretched, expanded into more dimensions, stopped howling. Now he is strong; he can throw me over his shoulder like a hide.

NORWAY 1941

Countdown

I watch my family while they sleep. I am an expert in silence and secrecy. I stand over their bodies, their mounds and hollows, and watch them twitch, stretch and furl. If they wake, they think I'm a dream. Tonight, I stand in Bjørn's bedroom, trying to work out where he might be.

The bedclothes are strapped tight across my brother's bed and there's a gap between the curtains the width of an eye. I push one of them aside. It's still dark. Opposite is the white shadow of the house my grandparents once lived in. They used to sit in their lounge upstairs, and I'd watch their silhouettes flutter in the candlelight. My goodnights used to be incomplete without a wave to my grandmother from my own bedroom; we'd blow our kiss to each other from the open windows, even in freezing midwinter, so that the kisses would rise and arc and meet between the two houses. 'The kisses are kissing,' I'd say to my mother, and in the morning I'd search the ground for them, for dints in the snow in winter, or white flowers in spring. But my grandparents have been dead for five years and now the ground between the houses is flat with grass.

I open Bjørn's wardrobe. Inside are stacks of folded clothes. I lie on my back on his bed and let my hands dangle over the sides.

I start counting down from a hundred.

At zero I promise myself I will tell our mother he has gone, and perhaps she will tell me where.

Norway 1941

Bear

Perhaps, in her bones, Caroline's mother already knows, as she wakes to the phantom turn of the door handle. Caroline is all ghost as she tiptoes in, the sound of her as pale as her hair. She crawls into her mother's bed, as though she is small again, bringing a chill with her. Her mother takes a breath.

'Bjørn has gone,' Caroline says. 'His bed is empty.'

Her mother does not let go of her breath, as though the ocean has closed above her. Her fingers, wrapped around her daughter, are pricking, hungry for oxygen. The silver fish travel through her wrists and up her arms; they are bound to reach her heart. *This must be the end of her.* She will go under for good. Her heart will explode with the pressure.

The room is black, even with her eyes open.

As black as inside her head when her eyes are closed.

Black out.

Black-out.

Out there, the black of the ocean, the same black as the sky. And dark dots of planes and black shadows of submarines, and perhaps searchlights, and a boat. *My black bear*, whispers Caroline's mother into her daughter's hair, which is the colour of cream roses.

'He'll come back,' Caroline says. Her mother's hands are cold and she doesn't reply.

THE NORTH SEA 1941

Open Water

'Name?'

'Bjørn.'

'Don't talk so loud. Sit.'

Tonight the boat is packed with men instead of fish. It holds twenty-three of us, but barely. Most of us sit below deck where it's as dark as pitch, the air salt-sharp. The fjord, beyond the frame of the boat, must be flat and calm. We are fed along it, waiting for the lurch of open water.

We press our backs against the wooden belly of the boat. Our knees and boots are racked in a line; we are not used to such proximity of bodies. That's what the war does: snap in half the distance we keep between us, and then in half again, and again, until there is a thigh either side of our own, another ear just inches away. We face people we cannot see.

There's a lunge and a dip, as the fjord gathers itself up and heaves us out. The waves greet us like a slap on the back from a drunken friend: *slap – we've been expecting you – slap – we've missed you – slap – don't rub us up the wrong way.*

Later, I spend dark hours on deck, as the knots slip past. We trawl just the one dimension, always forward; yet they could come at us from above, below, or anywhere across the curve of the earth. Although, down: we could also go down. There are shadows of ships on the horizon, but the harder I look, the more shadowy they become, until they are nothing but a trick of the dark.

We see the light of the first plane before we hear its engine; the others emerge from behind it, the three of them clattering through the clouds. The waves settle, just for a moment, as if waiting to see what is going to happen. The rain sleets across us, catching the beams from the aircraft and dashing them onto the deck, the wood dancing with drops and light.

The skipper sends us below deck; we drop through the hatch like fruit. We sit, back where we started, but now we are stiff with seawater, and beneath that, with fear. From down here, the storm drowns out the sound of the engines, until the wind drops and the sky gets louder. We close our eyes, hug our knees and wait.

Time ebbs, sinks, crests; when everything is black, nothing can be measured.

NORWAY 1941

Safekeeping

Because we are not allowed to talk about such things, I cannot ask Henrik if he knew that one day our son would be gone.

Did you know? I ask him, instead, in the ramming of the butter knife onto the table.

Were you in on it? I ask him in the tying of the too-tight knot in my apron.

Did you help him? I ask, a stone of a question inside the sweet flesh of a different question.

Might you have gone too? I ask with my hand, when I give him a note, pushed under the door to our house.

Couldn't you have told me? I ask him in the pause before I open the front door and smile at a young man who isn't our son.

Don't you miss him too? I ask him with my back, when I undress at night.

Do you think he's safe? I ask Henrik as he sleeps and as I stand outside Bjørn's room and listen to the breathing of another young man who is not our son.

Are we doing what's right? I ask him out loud, across Bjørn's bed, after another mother's son has left.

What do we tell Caroline? I ask. *She is so full of questions.*

Yes. Yes. No. No. No. Yes. Yes, he replies, with his eyes, hands, fingers, lips, a finger against lips; though perhaps his answers were not given in that order. I can't be sure.

Yes, he replies, with his mouth, and *Whatever keeps her safe.*

The North Sea 1941

The Relenting of the Storm

03:00

The storm is torn between the boat in the ocean and the planes in the air. There are men in boat and plane, the storm notes. It dances the waves like a puppetmaster. It could tie clouds around one craft like a blindfold and it could capsize the other with a flick. It could flood one with waves, with a single wave, and decorate one with lightning. The storm cannot decide between the men on the water and the men in the sky, and so it dilutes its threats, watching the aircraft slide away, towards where the sun will rise, and letting the waves collapse.

09:00

In the morning, the sky is blue, denying everything.

SHETLAND 1941

Ashore

Men are only part of the cargo. The letter Bjørn was under orders to carry is written on silk and sewn into the lining of his jacket; the message is spelled out in code. In the office, he takes the tip of a knife to the stitches and pulls out the fabric square. Despite the voyage, it's still dry, and a little warm. Bjørn holds it for a second, until it no longer contains his heat. The ink has bled into the grain of the weave.

Bjørn wonders how much it would have mattered, if all had been lost at sea. What difference would it make, what would change, what other lives would be lost or saved, if he and the letter sank without trace? How long would it have taken until the sea life ate the silk?

SHETLAND 1941

Lotion

'I will fetch something for your skin.' The woman touches Bjørn's outstretched wrist and peels open his fingers. He pulls his hand away; her skin is colder than his, her knuckles like rope knots.

'Wait there,' she says.

The usual building, used for men like him, ripe off the boat, is full tonight, and so they have brought him here, to this old woman. If he stands straight, his head will graze the ceiling.

The woman appears again, holding a tray of blue glass bottles and green glass jars, and a fold of muslin. The vessels shake against each other in time with her half-steps. The woman is called Daphne, a name he struggles to pronounce. She sets the tray on the table. On the mantelpiece, a candle gives a sigh, crackles and dies.

'Bjørn,' she says, as if it's a greeting in itself. She drips some lotion into her hand. 'This one is made from honey, and that one is cider vinegar.' She waits for him to offer his hands.

'No,' he says, instead. 'No thank you.' He pushes his hands into his pockets, trying not to wince as the rough fabric scours his skin. 'I'm tired.'

This is not what he had imagined. He had pictured a shared room, fellow Norwegians whom he may or may not have known. He had imagined hard, narrow beds, and Scottish whisky and sleep without dreams. He had expected salutes and orders, perhaps girls. He had not expected an old woman, a small cottage – someone's home. He cannot tell if the sound of the sea is coming from outside, or if it's in his head, a background noise from the last few days, or from the last few years – or perhaps from all his life, that he will never shake free. He feels like a boy, as always.

NORWAY 1941

Anagram

The basement is mostly a black space, with a small lantern in the corner and lines of light that shine through a trap door. It smells of damp wood, dry earth and peeling years of paint. Caroline picks out the letters of her name, in order, from her father's printing tray, and lays them on the table. She has been doing this since she was able to stand on her toes and reach her fingertips across the printing bench. The compartments of the wooden tray remind her of fields, each the right shape and size for what it needs to hold. When there were still five of them in the house, she would pick all the letters out for all their names - Caroline, Bjørn, Espen, Hilde and Henrik - and run up the stairs to the kitchen, shaking them in her cupped hands where they would leave ink laced across her palms. She would spread the letters out on the kitchen table and make new words, some real, some not.

She learned to read the letters in reverse, and sometimes she wrote them that way too. *Lots of children get the 'b', the 'd', the 'p' mixed up*, said her teacher. *But Caroline often writes the 'e' the wrong way round, the 's' and the 't'. She's making life difficult for herself*, she said, talking over the top of Caroline's head as she sat between her parents. *But life is difficult*, her father had said to the teacher. *There's nothing wrong with seeing things differently*. Later, at home, Caroline sat on his knee. He held a soup of letters in his hands. *If you can be the mirror for the words, if you can see them backwards and forwards, if you can imagine words as a physical thing, you will have a power over them that others don't.*

She spells her brother's name out loud as she picks out his letters. Later, while her parents sleep, she sews them into the hem of one of her dresses, as though she knows that, one day, her precious things will need to be carried with her.

SHETLAND 1941

Vection

Bjørn lies, eyes shut, on the old lady's spare bed in the blue dusk of the room, a knitted blanket itching like insects on the back of his neck. One foot is bare, the other booted; both are cold.

His body has forgotten that he is ashore, has been for sixteen hours. It is the dip and rise of the waves that still buoy him, not the mattress. He opens his eyes against the current of sleep and sits up, swinging his feet back onto the stone floor. He leans down to undo his bootlaces, but the action makes him dizzy. He stands instead, to try and rid himself of this new habit of motion, but still, beneath him, around him, is a swell and fall - inside him even. He wonders if the other men from the boat are also in their temporary beds, drifting and bobbing on an invisible tide.

He lowers himself onto the edge of the bed and lifts his boot to untie the laces, his fingers calculating the knot. The sea has swollen and stiffened the leather and when he pulls the boot off, the water has also shrivelled his skin, channelling it into its own set of waves. He tosses the boot to one side, regretting the slab of noise it makes, hoping he hasn't woken the old woman. The candle has nearly burned out, its light condensed to a glimmer in the corner. He peels his wet sock off, and for a second the motion stops; everything stops, and he is back at home in the depths of the night, pulling on that same sock, dry and clean.

But that was five days ago and this is only a lull; everything begins to shift again.

He slides his hand into the sock; the knit is colder and wetter than when it was on his foot. He feels for the four tiny blocks but can only find three, and he is seized by a panic that surges fast and high. He shakes the sock, and out flies the last block, landing under the bed. He holds the candle out to locate it, cupping the flame against draughts. The fourth printer's block, the letter m, has fallen in the gap between two floorboards. Bjørn flicks it out with his thumbnail. He places the four letters, like extracted teeth, on the mantelpiece in order:

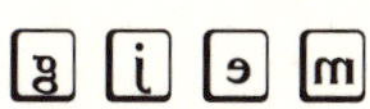

Home

He had taken the letters from his father's printing table in the ink-black basement the night before he left, sentimental and reckless.

He lifts his foot up; in the candlelight his sole is pale like fish-flesh, but there are fading pink indentations of the four letters. He hadn't felt the blocks between his foot and his sock as he'd walked down to the shore in the dead of night, when he'd rowed out into the water. He hadn't felt the letters digging in as he stood lookout, paced the boat, hauled and climbed and hid, nor as the sea had swept him off his feet, nor when the next wave, and the next, had kept him and all the other men down flat on the deck. The imprint had been so constant that he'd not noticed it at all.

SHETLAND 1941

Three Kinds of Sickness

The seasickness might pass quickly, in a matter of hours. Or for some unfortunate men, it might last for days, and it's on these occasions when it can mutate unnoticed into homesickness: this is less violent than seasickness, less wrenching, but no less physical. It travels through the blood, an eternal circuit. It's mild during the day, but surfs high at night. It stops sleep, tossing in the gut like a fish swallowed whole; and when the men do fall asleep at last, the past burrows into the present and hatches as a dream. Dreams flash the men back to the valleys or the coast or the bed of their wife or the lap of their mother; dreams crack open and fling them home.

Land sickness, or motion sickness, now that one's a trick: a trick of the ocean, to remind us where we came from; a trick of the present, feeding off the past – the destination clinging to the journey.

One day, you might wake, and all will have passed.

SHETLAND 1941

Lotion II

Daphne wakes; a boy is crying, and she remembers what this is like. For a second, time has folded, and she is thirty-five again. But in the moment it takes for her eyes to adjust, time has opened out again; this is someone else's son crying.

Before she goes to his bedroom, she fetches the tray from the kitchen, placing a candle among the bottles. She enters his room without knocking and sits on the edge of his bed. Taking one of his unresisting hands, she spreads the cream in waves, from his lower arm to the ends of his fingers.

'Are these splinters?' She peers at his hand, rubbing her finger across the raised slips of wood under his skin.

'Yes,' he whispers. 'Rope burns too, I think.'

She lifts a starched lid from another jar. 'Shetland lavender,' she says, sniffing it. 'In oil and beeswax.' She dips her fingers in and with the cream she dabs the burns; already there are scabs at the edges of them, and lines of salt-water blisters. 'When did you leave Norway?'

'Five days ago.'

'Were you frightened, crossing the ocean at night? Those fishing boats are not meant for that kind of journey.'

He looks down at his hands in the shadows cast by the flame, as though they belong to someone else. 'Some boats don't make it.'

'I know.' Daphne rubs the last smear of cream into her own hands. 'The honey will draw out the splinters, and the lavender will work on the burns.'

'I couldn't stay there.' Bjørn sits up in the bed, using his elbows to push himself against the headboard. 'At home. I had to do something more.'

'You are going to London tomorrow?'

'Yes. For training. There won't be many more boats making the trip. The nights will be too short soon; there will be too much light.'

'What about your mother?'

The candle begins to dance, as though the air in the tiny room has been disturbed.

'She has my younger sister,' he says. 'Caroline. And my older brother lives nearby. He is a teacher.'

'Who knows that you left on the boat?'

'My father will suspect.'

'You're not a fisherman?'

'A printer. Like my father. But I can handle a boat, of course.'

Daphne returns the bottles to the tray, one by one.

'I had a son, once.' She places the man's hand back on the bed. 'Your mother will be proud of you. One day, you will return to her.'

NORWAY 1942

Olfaction

We were used to men coming to stay. I wasn't allowed to ask questions. 'Your cousin Ola is coming to stay tonight, Caroline. Just for one night,' I was told, the first time, after Bjørn left. 'I don't have a cousin Ola,' I'd replied. 'Yes. You do.' These 'cousins' came and went: Lars, Sverre and Knut. And even at fourteen, I knew they weren't Lars, Sverre or Knut; I tested them, calling their name and waiting for the sliver of delay before they remembered to answer.

They slept in Bjørn's room; they gave it a use. Sometimes they wore his clothes, too, the next day, and as they walked down to the edge of the fjord, they could have been him. My job was to make the bed the next day and tidy up after them, though none of them made a mess.

Each left their smell in the bed, and I'd get in and lie on my back under the blankets before I neatened them out. Each time there was a fraction less left of Bjørn; each time he was a little more gone. And the space in my heart that missed him inhaled the sweat and sleep and youth of the men who came to stay for a night. Men had different cores, I decided, and their bodies betrayed them while they slept. Sometimes, the bed smelled of plant-life, undergrowth, wet and dark. Other times it was animal, smelling of musk and running. Or I'd lie under the blankets and breathe in the scent of wood, freshly carved, and I'd picture the harboured man lying here the night before, the woodgrain running top to toe, planed wide at knees and chest.

When Arne came, I broke the rules. As he sat at our kitchen table, eating thoughtfully, as though it were his last meal, I asked a question. 'Arne?' I pointed to his collar. 'Why do you have a paperclip on your shirt?' He put his spoon down and touched the clip, as though he'd forgotten it was there. He twisted it off and placed it on the table, pushing it closer to me.

'Line,' he said, changing my name to two syllables from the four-syllable *Car-o-lin-e*. No one had ever done that.

'They have banned our symbols.' He spoke to me as if my parents were not there, sitting at the table with us. 'But banning symbols is like trying to bail out water from a boat. You get rid of this much.' He held his cupped hands out together, like an offering.

'And the same amount gets back in somewhere else.' He picked up his spoon again and pointed it at me. 'Why do you think we chose a paperclip?'

'It holds things together?' I said.

'Exactly.' He looked from my mother to my father, and back to me.

'On the collar, Line, is illegal.' He picked a book from the shelf behind him, and tucked the paperclip over some pages. 'This is fine. But, like this ...' He slid the clip from the pages and placed it again over his lapel, the sharp ends snagging the fabric. '*This* is illegal. There have been arrests for wearing this. There will probably be deaths, maybe have been already.' He pulled another paperclip from his pocket and held it out to me in his palm. 'Hold your hand out and close your eyes.'

I did as I was told and for a second I felt the tickle of the clip on my palm. After that, my hand felt empty.

'It feels like you are holding nothing, yes?'

I nodded, still with my eyes closed.

'And yet that, in your hand, even though you can't feel it, makes the Germans so afraid, they will arrest you for wearing it. *That* is why we are more powerful.'

The next day, after Arne had gone, and my father pottered around the house with tired eyes, I went to Bjørn's room to make the bed. I lay under the blankets, but there was no smell of plant or wood or animal. I slid down, and bent my knees, tenting the covers, tucking them beneath my head, as though the dark would magnify my sense of smell; but there was nothing. It was an inert space. I got back out, annoyed for a reason I couldn't put my finger on, and picked up the pillow, ready to whack and shake. Lying beneath it was a pile of paperclips. I set the pillow on the floor and lifted up a clip; the rest followed, like a daisy-chain. I lowered it into my palm: a circle of them, the size of a bracelet, the size of my wrist.

NORWAY 1942

When the Day Comes

They will come, are coming, for the teachers. In the cities: Oslo, Bergen, Stavanger. In the towns, the villages, the hamlets, in the mountains, on the coast, rounding them up. The rumours that they are coming for them have blown, with the snow, over the hills into Espen's village for weeks. At night, he watches the shivery wick of moonlight cross the wall, listening, in case they come at night.

When they do come, they come by day. He sits on the edge of his bed and holds his breath, tracking the seconds by the thud of their boots outside. He hears them halt a few doors away, and his breath is a silent whistle from his lips.

His bedroom window is ajar and the outside drifts in, louder than the drum of his heart; the sea, behind the shoreline houses, cracks itself against the boats. The hills catch the wind and pitch it back again. He is homesick before he has left, and he tries to memorise the beat of the sea outside.

There's a slam of a limb, or a gun, on the front door.

There are feet on the stairs. Espen thinks about making his bed, but instead he ties his shoelaces, his fingertips stumbling over the knot. He curses; he knows knots, all kinds. Two of the men are in his room now, yapping orders. A clenching fear squeezes the air in the room – their fear, and his. One of the officers pushes him in the small of his back as he walks down the stairs, as though the man has somewhere better to be.

Outside, the air is sharp and cold and salt; Espen's breath is already a scatter of ice. They take away his coat. They have brought the teachers from other villages, and they herd them into the road. Folk line the way ahead, silhouettes against a low, blinding sun. The snow is golden, scattered with grey shadows where feet have been. The footprints all look the same, thinks Espen, the teachers' and the soldiers'.

NORWAY 1942

Hushed

Staying still is something I have become good at. If they come for us, I shall stay still, like a good girl. I'll pretend to be too scared to move, to speak. My parents and I practise being quiet; we rehearse silence. There are many kinds of quiet. Sometimes there seems to be just one, and that kind, it crushes – the silence I imagine being pushed upon you by an avalanche. Sometimes the quiet is layered, like the snow in the village: dense, light, packed, drifting up against our houses, insulating our walls. There are old silences, like the one when Espen used to read and I'd lie on his bed, frozen-still so I didn't disturb his concentration. There are regular, repetitive silences, like the quiet of the first October snowfall, a change that you hear from beyond the shutters, before you see it through the window. Then there are the new kinds of quiet, like the one when we listen for footsteps, bootsteps, the one when we wait for knocks like hail on the door, and the powdery one when they have passed our house and we breathe again. The quiet blanket when all three of us pretend to be asleep. The icy silence after a question. The quiet when the printing press in our basement stops, when the din – its clatter and swipe and jerks – stops and everything left over seems like silence, until your ears adjust. The quiet of the fjord in the dark, Bjørn waiting. The hush of not being told the truth.

The quiet when I am the only child who is left.

NORWAY 1942

Evidence

Espen's front door is open and as I walk up the stairs, my nose tells me my son is here. The leather of his boots, the vinegar sweat of his feet, the chalk of his hands, the soap in his thick hair, which never quite rinses clear.

My ears tell me he is here. The cat he feeds follows me in, yowling, its claws impatient on the wood of the stair treads. Upstairs, from his room, I hear the hiss of a radio, leaking interference.

I pick up his coat, halfway up the stairs. He must be here, because he wouldn't leave without his coat. It's heavy, like an animal, and the wool is rough on my cheeks when I bury my face in its folds.

At the top of the stairs, I wait before opening the door. The handle is brass and cold; the radio is too loud. I close my eyes and see the child he used to be, the yellow scar on his back that grew across as he grew tall. I feel his black eyelashes on my cheek. I hear his footsteps, whose weight and pace I would know among a hundred other pairs. I smell the radiance of his sunburnt skin in August.

I open the door to his bedroom and see, through the static sound and the creak of the hinges and the smell of his slept-in tangle of bedclothes trailing on the floor, that what I heard is true.

Absence makes an echo, too.

NORWAY 1942

Scars

'Try to make a memory for each season,' a voice says as we rattle along the train tracks, standing nose to back, like cattle.

Summer

I think of my sister Caroline, as blonde as I and Bjørn are dark, as blonde as our mother. One summer, she patrolled the garden for fallen bees, poor, slow things, emptied of energy, and she fed them honey water. She'd crouch, her brown shoulders hunched, the bees flying off while she was looking elsewhere.

Spring, or autumn

I think of Bjørn, nine or ten, cracking open the April ice, and extracting the limp, hide-brown autumn leaves, one at a time, drying them on the stove until they were crisp enough to dissolve to dust. He collected the dust in a glass jar, layers and layers, years of autumns, years of springs.

Winter

I think of my mother, her belly big enough to burst, embroidering by candlelight, her eyes watering, sucking on a pierced finger. 'Caroline,' she said. 'Your sister will be called Caroline.' None of us asked how she knew. She sewed my sister's name, twisted with flowers and fruit and vines. My sister came early, and my mother hadn't quite finished.

One morning

I think of my father, his fingers taking mine, rolling them across the black inkpad, and then the paper, over and over. We looked at my prints, the lines and non-lines, and I could never believe that they wouldn't ever change, only get bigger. I chopped them into squares and kept them in a tin, evidence of me.

The problem is – I find – the past is the skin, and the memory is the cut, and one day, you just want it all to heal.

NORWAY 1942

Senses Six to Ten

6. Temperature

The leather handles of the nut-coloured suitcase are warm in Caroline's hands, skin on skin, as are the floorboards she kneels upon. She takes off her coat; she wants to feel the chill from the open window. If her brother is cold, wherever he is, she will be cold too, in his bedroom.

7. Direction

From the window, Caroline watches her mother walk the road outside. Each time she leaves Caroline's line of sight, she changes direction and returns into view, strides past the building, and disappears again. She looks straight ahead, and walks like there is something on her heels.

8. Balance

Caroline stands at the top of the stairs, Espen's suitcase next to her. His initials stamped on the side – E.P.H. – bring her vanished brother closer. In the case are his belongings: jumpers that smell of him, soft balls of socks, books, pens, maps, photographs of birds and insects, blurry in flight, a tin of smudgy fingerprints. His watch. She cannot lift the suitcase down the stairs by herself.

9. Time

'What will he do without his watch?' Caroline asks.

'He will find other ways of telling the time,' her mother says. 'Sometimes it's better not to know how much time has passed.'

Caroline counts the seconds and the steps as she and her mother carry the suitcase down the stairs, a handle each. One step; one second. At the bottom, she waits for her heart to find its pace.

'It's in us anyway,' Caroline says. 'Time's in us, even if watches made us forget.'

10. Place

Caroline pins up one of her brother's maps on her bedroom wall and places her finger on an area of green, lacking in symbols. Her finger slides up a little, like a shoe on ice. 'North,' she says. 'He's north.'

NORWAY 1942

Tract

The pigs make a noise like the shluck of iron under the blacksmith's hammer. The cows are quiet, although if we were close we would surely feel their snorts of panic – hot, damp, condensing on our cheeks. The German soldiers are guttural and angry. They stab the earth with their guns, as if they hate the land itself. They spit noisily, then grind their boots, making sure part of them will be left behind. They have whipped and kicked the cattle into a pen, and the cows are turning, rumps against heads, tails jerking, ears alive, restless with this final, sudden event.

They line us up, men and boys. We watch. They make us watch.

The chickens know this is no fox, but they run and scatter just the same, claws tearing at the ground, not yet headless. Soon their eggs will rot, uncollected.

When the animals are dead, we wonder if we will be next, whether they will corral us into the pen, whether we will be as quiet as the cattle. In one of the houses, a dog barks, as though it is sobbing. It is a rogue sound; the soldiers want to be the noise-makers, they want to hear their orders dropping like pins on glass. One of them breaks away to hunt the dog.

Some of us had harboured the agents; some of us pretended not to see, but the soldiers had jabbed and tugged us all, regardless, from houses, barns, boats and jetties, and now we are an untidy line, from sixteen to sixty, with fish scales under our fingernails, salt in our skin, and the unknown in our throats. The spring chill is sucking at our earlobes, fingertips and collarbones. Alongside us are trees, not yet in leaf, and among their roots stand our women and children, looking for their husbands and fathers and brothers and sons, but we close our eyes, afraid for them. Somewhere in our ragged audience, one of us coughs, again and again, trying to hold it in, sounding like a choke now. None of us look.

The soldiers make us turn to the fjord, make us walk towards the shoreline. They direct us with gun barrels, levering them back and forth through the air.

The sinking of the boats takes longer than the slaughter of the livestock.

They make us watch.

The boats hulk into the water, leaning and keeling, the masts pointing at us, shrinking, sinking. Fishing nets float on the surface of the water, sitting like grids until they sink too. We wait for the moment when each boat capsizes, lurching, bellying seawater. The flip, when it comes, from upright to over, is almost a relief. One by one by one – *tip, tip, tip* – the last few breaths of our livelihoods. After the last ripple reaches shore, a shot echoes back to us, mid-bark.

We do not watch our homes exploding around us. Instead we watch the dust jump from the ground onto our boots; or we shut our eyes, the noise and the choking smoke branding shadows of our houses onto the inside of our lids for us to keep. We vibrate together, from the ground up; and long after the explosions cease, the rage still trembles through our limbs. A fire engulfs each plot, singeing the hairs on the back of our hands, and for days we will lift our hands up and smell what they have done.

When there is nothing left, they send orders and boats. 'Walk,' they shout, and we walk; we breathe air charged with dynamite and tread death-sodden land. They will remove its name from their maps. It is a village without houses, animals, people. There are no walls, no boats, no roofs. It is rubble and blood and broken belongings, and our risk and fight lie in the shallows. But as we walk past the trees, past our women, to the shore and onto their boats, a tract of the village is pulled through each of us. A common origin and destination. It sits fallow in us, through the interrogation, to the camps; we drag it through the hope and out the other side, and take it with us into our own deaths.

It will pull us back, though, some of us. On the way home, with ribbons for ribs and with death burning in our mouths, we will begin to dream of tending and founding. We will buy tools in Sweden that hang heavy in our wasted arms, and we will build our homes again. Our grandchildren will swim in the fjord. 'Watch,' they will shout, and we will watch them.

NORWAY 1942

Undoing

'Take it off, Caroline,' my mother says quietly. She makes a ring around her wrist with her thumb and finger, showing me what she means.

'No one can see it,' I whisper, and hold my right hand over the cuff of my left. The loops of metal around my wrist are blood-warm.

'Give it to me.'

It would surely be worse to remove it now, with the soldiers everywhere. 'I want to keep it on.'

'Give it to me now, Caroline. If they find it on you ...'

Erik, who is only eight, is crying into his mother's apron and she is trying to muffle him, stuffing the fabric into his mouth. Butterflies of charred fabric dance past us, tumbling towards the fjord or sucked high into the wind, black dots against the sky, which is bright and blue, as if it doesn't care that everything has gone.

I feed my paperclip bracelet out of my sleeve, scratching tracks along the skin. I slip my hand into my mother's and the bracelet sits between our palms. A passing, plodding soldier looks at us, holding hands. He stops and comes close, the heat of his breath on my throat. He reaches to touch my hair, and my mother lifts her free hand as though she's going to stop him. He smiles something that isn't a smile, and walks on.

When she lets go of my hand, my palm is empty.

'Don't look at me,' she says, but I do.

Her hands are busy behind her back. She is pulling the paperclips apart, yanking them so that the shapes tear from each other. She tosses each twisted spear backwards into the ferns. The leaves are not yet fully uncurled from winter, and I hope the sun doesn't catch the metal strewn beneath them. I move a little to the side and give them my shadow.

The soldier is coming back; I hate this one more than all the others. My mother takes me by the hand again. He stops in front of us, leans on his gun and says something in German. She lifts her hand to tuck a strand of hair behind her ear. I see it, and the soldier sees it too: a crooked paperclip, caught on a thread of my mother's sleeve, dangling, catching the sun.

NORWAY 1942

Maturation

I wait for a gunshot from the woods, picture my mother falling, body into skirt into dirt.

But what I hear behind me is the sound of steps, crushing the ground; they are hers, and behind hers are his: slow, satisfied. She takes her place next to me again, and also takes my hand, her skin cold, holding it just like she had done earlier, as though she'd never been gone for those ten minutes, never left me standing alone, with my back to the woods. The air warms in the small void between her palm and mine, and hardens like a nut.

The soldier walks around us, smiling something that isn't a smile. I think not of my mother, but of the nuts we studied at school, peeled and dissected: *pericarp*, from the wall of the ripened ovary; *exocarp*, the outer layer; *endocarp*, sometimes woody, sometimes just a membrane, a lining.

Our palms are stiff with lines: love, head, life.

As the soldier peels away down the path to the fjord, he throws silver from his hand. A ruined, undone paperclip lies in the dirt at our feet. My mother bites her lip until she breaks the skin. She drops my hand to wipe her mouth; her nails are black with bark, and the blood spreads thin on the back of her hand, drying like berry juice.

NORWAY 1943

Learning to Share

There's enough to go around, we tell the little ones at mealtimes. But there's not enough of anything to go around. There are not even enough mothers to go around; not enough arms, or laps.

All the children have something they won't let go of. After the boats had gone, loaded with our husbands, fathers, cousins, brothers, sons, uncles, nephews, grandfathers, we'd poked the ashes of what used to be our homes with sticks, rescuing anything that could still be recognised. Most recovered things we gave to the children.

/ A chewed pencil, pitted with Tomas's father's teeth marks.

/ A collection of buttons, two big, two small, that are now a family of four for little Marit Hanssen to play with.

/ A doll's blanket, because once the smoke and charred dust are shaken out, it smells of home. All the little ones try to claim it, and we explain about sharing.

/ A wooden teacup, carved, scraped and hollowed before you were born, and later painted with your name, in white, *Caroline*, decorated with cherries. Although you are not one of the little ones, not any more.

Some things that we find, we keep for ourselves.

\ A shred of a *bunad* made by our grandmother, or great-grandmother. The ash-black wool, a bodice, or a hem, hard and heavy with embroidery – bold-coloured wreaths of flowers tendrilled from thread.

\ A pewter candle holder, tossed from a house with the first blast, and still lined with wax that melted while we shared our last meal.

\ Half a book, a front cover, the spine tattered with broken grid-threads. A new last page.

\ A pebble from our garden, because it's older than any of us, older than any of this.

We all live together, and we learn to share. Food, space, clothes, children, disease, stories, hope, lice, toys, mothers. No one fights over the doll's blanket now; it smells of all of us. Little Anna has it to herself, tucked in the crook of her elbow as she sucks her thumb, looking up to see whose knee she is sitting on.

Waiting

If we are not doing, we are waiting. There is nothing in between.

We wait for:

News
Signs
Symbols
Boats
The storm
Landfall
Nightfall
The taken
The found
Soldiers
Attack
Orders
Retreat
Daybreak
Noises
Quiet
Peace
The end

NORWAY 1945

Sleep Patterns

My mother dreams of her eldest son's return so often that when he does appear, ragged and hollow, she doesn't believe what she can see, hear, smell, touch. She runs her hands up and down his sides, across his shoulders, patting as she goes, as though his skin no longer fits. She tells him that she has dreamed of this, and Espen tells her that he stopped dreaming years ago.

He lies, though. I watch him sleep and I see the roll and dart of his eyes beneath his lids. His breath is hot and fast. Years later, I will think of him, as my newborn babies learn to breathe, as though all the air in the room is not enough.

When his temperature creeps up, my mother sends me to fetch bowls of snow, which she packs onto his forehead. Her fingers turn red, and then white. The snow melts and runs down his temples like a stream down a mountain. I bring a fresh pillow and take the wet one away. I sit on a stool and dry it in front of the stove until my wrists ache.

The kitchen smells of hot feathers and damp cotton. The windows sweat.

Afterwards, we are told we must burn the bedding, but the feathers do not want to ignite, and the frozen ground does not want to be dug.

NORWAY 1945

Destined

Half our men are returning. It could have been the other half, or an entirely different fraction. Standing in my shoes, walking to the station, preparing to meet their husband, could have been Katje, Ellen or Guro. In Caroline's place could have been Erik or Anne, waiting for their father. It's down to a twist of fate. Ha. As though fate is flexible, mouldable, persuadable. Perhaps the boy Arne – who sat at our kitchen table and held out that paperclip, who took my Caroline's name and turned it into *Line … Lina* – was right; perhaps that little paperclip symbol means more than anyone realised. Maybe we tuck ourselves into that little steel loop, and we think it's so secure, wedging each page of our history into its clasp. And then, when we're not looking, the loop's wrenched open, the shape gone. Our pages swoop and fall, glide away. The steel is undone, the twist is done, and it's us, not them; them, not us (now the long, thin S – what for? *Self*? *Soldier*? *Son*? *Shame*? – Or maybe it's a 5, what once was our family: man, woman, boy, boy, girl). We are unclipped. Picked. Unpicked. Ticked. Unticked. Tick. Tock. The men are late, according to one of the clocks.

NORWAY 1945

Unification

We all sit around the edges of the station, on seats that have seen better days. Everything, everyone, has seen better days. A packet of cigarettes is passed around; we tap one out, and use the children to convey the packet along the line.

Caroline sits next to me, not a child any more. Our shoulders align, the same height, but her back is straighter, her breasts newer. When I pass her the cigarette packet, she keeps it for a moment too long, as if it holds an answer, or a question.

'No, Caroline. You're too young,' I say.

'I'm eighteen,' she says, but she sighs and hands the packet to Annette, sitting next in line. A soldier wanders past, lighting each of our cigarettes in turn. He, too, stops briefly at Caroline, before noting her empty hands, crossed on her lap.

We are beckoned to the platform. There's a clock above us, and one behind us. Their times conflict. Above the door it is three minutes to four; behind us, three minutes past. I wonder which is right, and whether it matters.

We hold our cigarettes to our lips and the smoke trails from our fingers. Our men arrive as silhouettes on the platform, crisp against the yellow station light. They huddle, as though each body needs the heat of the next, but they begin to disperse, feeding into a line in front of us. We remember to drop our cigarettes. We stub them out with the toes of our shoes, and wait for our men to recognise us.

NORWAY 1945

After the Station, the Hotel

The hotel is full of things I had forgotten existed. Portraits, unchipped glasses, paper napkins, moulded plaster, umbrella stands. Things whose use has persisted as intended – their purpose the same all these years later, all these seconds later, as when they were carved, whittled, constructed. They have fulfilled themselves, just as they are.

You see, where they sent us, where we, the women – and our children – have been kept, repurposing was a skill and a necessity. A loose thread was pulled, stitches unplucked, and unravelled into a skein around fingers, placed into the scrap-bag, ready for use again, for sewing or to be soaked in oil for a wick. Cups without handles became bowls. Wax was caught and melted again, and again; mixed and melted, remoulded. Old shoes became buttons; blunt scissors chewed the leather into circles, a sharp, unnamed piece of metal used to punch four holes. We were repurposed too, each morning, into whatever was needed: mother, nurse, cook, farmer, teacher.

The hotel is full of things I had forgotten existed. The touch of a finger against my cheek, the pause before a lie, his smell, blond hair on his arms, the future.

NORWAY 1947–1951

Background Noise

Hammering. Sawing. Mallets. Orders. Laughs. Cries. The chink of a nail held between teeth. Boots. Oars. Birdsong. Hinges being tested. The crack of a knuckle. The creak of bark. A dog. The sizzle of a wick. Iron singing. Songs. Iron shrinking. Chickens clucking, eggs dropping. The crack of a trunk. The split of the grain. Threshing. Kneading. Planing. Planting. Carving. Moulding. The heavy drip of metal. Waves. The clack of knitting needles. The chant of the pattern. The snip of scissors. Earth. A bee unwinding across a path. The brush and push of paint. The yelp of a rivet. The cries of babies. The slush and pull of milk in a bucket. The batter of rain. A beak in seed. The stamp of children. The gather and throw of leaves. The ticks of clocks. The winding of watches. A quiet swallow. Chalk on a board. The scrape of chairs. The turn of pages.

NORWAY 1951

Out of Nowhere

'Goodnight, Caroline.'

'Goodnight, Marit.' She is the last child to flit down the school-room steps. I stack the books on the desk. It's dark already, and the lights of the newly built homes reflect and waver in the fjord.

I pull down my hat, which I had felted from old jumpers, an activity to pass the time. It is a short walk home but my breath will harden on the wool of my scarf by the time I'm halfway there. I stand on the top step, stamped clean of snow by the children's feet, and pull the door closed.

There's a man on the path. His eyes are white, his other features shadows. I try to place him. I did this a lot when the men first came back; they came in a crowd, each one vaguely familiar, like relatives of themselves. The posture, the swing of the hammer, the stance – it was hard to tell who was who, and we declared their names when we spoke to them, over and over, as though they might need reminding who they were: 'Good morning, Anders. You're looking well, Anders.' Or: 'Nice work, Olav. Soon, Olav, that fence will be done.'

'Hello,' I say to the man as I join him on the path.

'Hello, Line.'

He pulls his scarf down, away from his face, and slides off one of his gloves. In his hand is a glint, a chain of links curled up on his palm, all kinds of silver – metal and ice and moon: 'This time,' he says, 'I have brought you a real bracelet.'

'You have come all this way?' I think of the crooked paperclips buried somewhere in the undergrowth, like hopeless seeds. 'The village is nearly rebuilt.' I point over his shoulder. 'And there are boats here again.'

Arne holds his hand out towards me, the bracelet looped over his fingers.

'And a church, Arne,' I say. 'They built a new church. I'm getting married there. Next month.'

ENGLAND

The Names we Use, and All Those we Don't

I change my name overnight. From my mouth, it sounds the same, but on paper it's different. Just one letter, and it looks like a whole other word. Arne had always called me Line, never Caroline. But in England, they'd looked at me, and then my name, on paper. *Your name is Line?* But they say it to rhyme with *fine*. No, I laugh. Of course not. Not like fine. Like Tina, or Gina. Line.

So, I change my name. I become Lina. Carolina. For a while it looks strange, foreign, make-believe – a different shape. Some people still rhyme it with *finer*. Like the US state.

I overhear Arne, on the phone, or in the pub. *You can call me Alec*, he says, as though people are incapable. *Banana*, is all he says to me, and grins. *It's the only thing in English that rhymes with it.*

When we have our children, their names must be a bridge, pronounceable by both their teachers in England and their grandparents back home. They should sound the same in both places, we decide, as my belly grows and my skin stretches and my ankles swell. No th. No å, ø or æ. No w or v. No j. Vowels are tricky; they glide from long to short between the languages.

In England, Liv is said like *Live*, not *Leave*.

We agree that the name of my grandfather, Odd, is impossible, although Arne smiles and says that Roar would be excellent.

We decide on Thomas and Kristin. Perhaps we would have decided on them at home, too. Perhaps not.

My mother sends them pencils, stamped along the side with their full names: neat, gold letters pressed into the paint, red for Kristin, green for Thomas. He doesn't like green, but my mother's not to know that. She embroiders letters for Kristin's bedroom wall and stitches them onto rope like bunting. She paints a picture of a boat for Thomas, and styles his name up the side. In their bedrooms, they are each surrounded by their own name, as though they might be in danger of forgetting it.

When my mother writes to me, she uses my real, full name. 'Good morning, Caroline,' the postman says, reading the envelope, pronouncing it the

English way. I don't correct him. He moves to a different route, or a different job, or a different city, and the new guy is more careful. 'Good morning, Mrs Madsen,' he says, handing me a parcel.

'A parcel from Grandma?' the children ask, jumping for a look.

'Yes.'

'Can we have the stamp?' Their fingers are already picking at the riddled edges.

'Wait,' I say. 'We need steam to remove it safely.'

They are more excited about the stamp than the contents of the package. 'What's it about?' they ask, as they glue it in their notebook, as though there's a whole story contained in the little square from across the sea.

Norway 1955

Heartwood

I knew, when he came back for Caroline, waiting for her in the shadows of the school house, that Arne would leave and take her with him. I saw it, actually, when he placed that paperclip into her fifteen-year-old palm across our kitchen table and made it disappear, when he shortened her name to *Line*.

I watched from the kitchen window as she broke the news to Olav, sitting on a fallen log near the water. When she returned to the house, her fingers were stained with the green juice of plants. Olav married someone else, in the end, just two months after he was to have married Caroline. As I stand at the sink, scrubbing the potatoes, the black soil-water running over my hands, I watch Olav's children scuttle past and imagine what they would have looked like if they'd been half ours. Blonder, maybe. Olav's mother has never forgiven me, ridiculous woman – as if I wouldn't have given anything for Caroline to stay.

I dry my hands. 'Henrik,' I shout. He is in his study, the room with the great north-facing window, the thin light, perfect for studying butterflies.

I hear him approach the kitchen, his limp louder on the wood floor of the hall.

'Can you post this parcel to Caroline?' I say. 'I'd like her to get it before the twins' birthday, and it will take a while to get to Cambridge.'

'How old are they?'

'Two. You know that, Henrik.'

He makes a noise from his throat, solid as regret. He picks up the parcel and tucks it under his arm.

'Don't rush. Take your time. Take care.'

I watch him from the front door; he holds his hip as though it's a child, troublesome, but loved. We are not old, but we feel aged. Henrik jokes that we are heartwood. 'Old and dead?' I ask him. 'Strong,' he replies.

When he's gone, I sit on the porch. There aren't many quiet moments like this. In our little village, there aren't many errands to run. The wood beneath my feet is old; it was salvaged from *before* – there are still charred shadows in patches, and parts where the black edges of the boards are lined and creviced like ancient knuckles, or lips. This original wood is greyer than the rest of the house, its rings older and harder. It's eight years since I watched Henrik fell the trees in the nearby woods. I'd marked each of them with a gash of red paint. I knew exactly which one the soldier had pushed me up against, which section of bark had scratched the skin between my shoulder blades, and the place either side of the trunk where my fingernails had dug into it. But I'd needed more than the one tree to go. All the others, that I'd counted back and forth, over his shoulder that thudded against mine, until it was over, they had to come down too. Henrik did as I asked. He stripped the bark and sliced open the trunks, roots to neck. He split them over and over into planks, trimmed and sanded them, until I was happy. We claimed those trees. They are layered into our rebuilt house; there are some in the kitchen, and in the *stue*. They clad our bedroom too, their grain like frozen waves. Henrik sanded them so well that when I lie in bed in the dark and pull my fingers across their surface, they feel like skin.

In the clearing, there are saplings.

NORWAY 1955

Teacher

He stands at the front of the class, as he has done ever since Caroline left. The children have pretty much forgotten her. They are his class now. On the second row sit his own girls, one at either end.

It's August, the beginning of the school year, and there are some new children. He keeps his name on the blackboard for them, large, like a label. BJØRN. The chalk dust has collected on the floor and he smudges it away with his boot. There's a dog barking somewhere outside, but it's so regular, no one notices it after a while.

He leads the children outside; they are to create pictures from sticks, flowers, leaves, whatever they can find. One of them picks up a dead insect. Go for it, Bjørn tells him, and the boy places it in his box. The children move together in a vague group, but wander and drift, a flock; they hold a map in their heads. Bjørn watches them, their heads down, backs rounded, concentrating like bees. They carry their boxes like treasure, placing them gently on the ground while they inspect their finds.

'Time's up,' calls Bjørn and the children line up, each holding a makeshift cardboard tray littered with materials. There are shards of bark shedding tree-dust, leaf skeletons, sticks peeled clean – white-green and cold. There are fresh pine needles and sharper, dead, brown ones, bruised petals, the tight tips of ferns, heathers and evergreens, sprigs of lilac and violet, and even a snail shell, light as paper. As Bjørn inspects the row of offerings, he picks out the end of a cigarette and a sweet wrapper and puts them in his pocket. There is a gleam of steel in one of the trays.

'Can I use them, Bjørn? Am I allowed?' The girl looks from her tray to Bjørn. 'It's not nature but …'

Bjørn pokes his finger into her collection and nudges the greenery to the side.

'Where did you come across these?'

Rikke points to an area behind her. 'Just there, in the ferns.'

'Well,' Bjørn says, 'we are supposed to be using natural materials only.'

'I could use both. I have an idea.'

The children are quiet and busy. The class is supposed to be moving on to history this afternoon, but Bjørn lets them carry on. They are careful, fingers pecking between their trays and their paper. History can wait until tomorrow.

The children's hands are skinned with dried glue, and the classroom smells of outside. Some of the pictures are abstract, and some are faces, or whole animals. Bjørn stops at Rikke's desk.

'Ready?' she says. Bjørn nods. She picks up her creation, lifting it from its tangle on the table. Rikke has made a mobile; it is almost as tall as she is. She has chosen carefully: leaves that are already dead but that don't crumble; sticks wide enough to put a hole through, but that aren't too heavy; stems, flexible but strong, clumped into expert knots, the knots of a fisherman's daughter. Linking all the pieces together are paperclips, untwisted, used as hooks or bent into loops. She hands Bjørn her work of art; her nails are broken and her fingertips are red with the bending.

'Great idea, Rikke.' Bjørn holds the mobile up for the rest of the class to see.

'Where do you think they came from, Bjørn?'

He looks at the slight pieces of metal. 'Who knows.'

After all the children but his own have gone home, Bjørn pins the children's the artwork to the wall. His daughters glue back on all the eyes, tails and fronds of hair that have dropped to the floor.

'Are we going to Grandma's on the way home?' they ask.

'Sure, we can say hello.'

Bjørn hangs Rikke's mobile in the window, where it turns in an unfelt draught, the steel sparking in the almost-autumn sun.

ENGLAND 1958

Resemblance

For the first month of his life, my son Thomas looked like my husband.

It took us by surprise when, at five weeks old, Thomas changed into my brother. Not big Bjørn, my living bear of a brother, but Espen, the eldest one, the one who strung us all together, who left for the concentration camp and came back too weak to fight a fever. My baby's flat, new nose became a little pointed; his eyes went from tiny and blue to large and brown. There was my brother's thin, ducky upper lip and his ears, pointed like an elf. The dimple in his chin, only noticeable when the light fell a certain way.

When she was two, three, four, Kristin would catch me watching her brother, as he hunched over his toy cars, or soared round the garden with a cape, sliding the willow tree branches through his fingers as he ran, and she would yank at my attention, tug at my clothes, hair, fingers. She learned to become adorable and patient. Sometimes she would nestle into me on a chair, as though she was trying to become me, infiltrate me, and she would cup my face in her little-girl hands, turning it towards her own. Sometimes I would shout the wrong name: Espen. Their twin heads would turn, disturbed. 'Who?' one of them would ask. One of them would bring me a pear from our tree, perfumed and softly bruised.

When we sent photographs home to my mother, we chose the blurry ones, or ones where Thomas was half hidden by Kristin. We put off taking them to my parents' house. *Arne's work. The snow. The twins' school. The weather. The twins have chickenpox – we think. The snow. Money. Actually, the weather.*

Espen's hair had been wavy and wild; it would attract sticks and burrs, and when he stood at the front of his classroom, strands of it glinted red in the midwinter's brief midday sun that lit him from the window behind. And now, Espen's hair grew from my son's head, faster than Kristin's blonde hair, which was really my hair, slow-growing and fine. When the twins were five, we ran out of excuses. On impulse, we shaved Thomas's head. He was brave at the barber's, although Kristin squeezed his hand too hard, holding his stare in the mirror, her tears landing among the wet chunks of hair on the linoleum floor. We took a photograph for his new passport, there and then, in the barbershop chair. He was sturdy, determined. I knew the look and my mother would know it too.

'I need a photograph as well,' Kristin said, tucking her blonde hair behind her ears.

As I paid, the barber slid a Cellophane packet across the counter, in it a lock of hair. I held it up to the sun, where it glowed red.

'It will grow again, won't it?' one of the children asked.

'Of course,' I said. 'So quickly.'

But it never grew so wavy, or so wild, again.

Pine

'That one,' says Thomas, pointing. 'The one with the yellow tag.'

'The yellow ones are too small for our living room,' I say. 'We need one with a blue tag.' Thomas's shoulders drop, and he moves closer to his chosen tree.

'This one, Mummy?' calls Kristin, her red mitten tugging at the end of a branch. Arne and I stand back, our arms folded, mid-decision. The rain has collected at the ends of the pine needles, millions of tiny beads capturing the white of the floodlights.

'That one, then?' I say. 'Sure?'

Kristin nods, stroking the tree's branches, like she does our cat's tail.

I wave the man over. 'We'll take this one please.'

Kristin finds a slip of a branch and hands it to me. I hold it under my nose, searching for a scent I might recognise. English pine smells different – soft, musty. The man pulls our chosen tree towards us. Like all the rest, its branches are spindly, the needles a pale, frosty grey – but at its heart it is darker, a shadowy green, as if that part remembers the hillsides and the thinner air.

I'm fourteen and a man is staying with us, a stranger. One afternoon, my father calls me. 'Caroline – come and help us.' I pull my boots on. The snow is falling so fast that their footprints have already been buried, and I make new ones, following my father's voice.

In the dark behind our house, I find the three men – my father, the stranger and Bjørn; they are carrying a pine tree. Its trunk lies along their shoulders, and their heads are bent, the snow gathering on their necks. The air smells of ice and sawdust and sap.

'How old is it?' I ask.

My father pats the trunk. 'About your mother's age.' He looks up and smiles at me through the branches. 'You want to help carry it?'

I walk towards him with high, big steps, leaving punctures in the thick drifts, and he holds a hand out for me, leaning, as though I'm adrift.

'Can you reach?' he asks, and I lift my arms up; we march across the snow back to the house. Flakes settle on my eyelashes, and I squeeze my eyes to melt them. Later, we will decorate the tree with candles and flags, and we will not know that such things cannot last.

We stand on Trafalgar Square, a tiny congregation of four. People move around us, dividing, sliding past. Some look at us, and then look at the tree, as though they hadn't noticed it before.

'It's pretty big,' says Thomas, his neck craning. It's cold for London;. Despite the fumes and the breathing of the crowds, it feels like it may snow.

'It won't snow,' says Arne. 'Sleet maybe.'

'How tall is it?' asks Kristin, unable to appreciate the tree's beauty without a scaffolding of facts. She stares up at it, as though trying to analyse the height, and her blonde hair, darker these days, falls straight down her back. The tree's lights reflect in her eyes, a cluster of reds and yellows.

'They've never missed a year,' says Arne. 'Each year Norway sends us a tree.'

'You mean *we* send *London* a tree,' I say. He looks at me. 'Yes. Or that.'

'We know, Dad.' Thomas turns away, to look at other things. 'You tell us every year.'

'How do they get it here?' asks Kristin.

'Cargo ship,' I say. I miss taking her hand in mine when I answer one of her many questions.

Thomas links my arm. 'Shall we go?' He looks up and holds his hand out, palm up. 'Hey, Mum, you were right. It's snowing.'

NORWAY 1958

Muscle Memory

'Don't come in winter,' my father had said. 'Why would you come in winter?'

'The children want to see the snow,' I said into the telephone, waiting for my voice to reach him, waiting for his to come back.

'It's be dark. They won't be able to see anything. Come in the summer. The children will be able to swim then.' The miles were silent between each sentence.

The plane circled, snow blustering past the windows. We prowled the sky, catching glimpses of the town beneath cloud. After an uncountable number of round, slow minutes, we couldn't land and the plane took us off back to Oslo, its engines roaring in apology.

The next day, it tried again. We shook, Arne holding my hand, all of us holding our breath, as the wheels of the plane trenched the ice-packed runway, coming jaggedly to a halt. It was mid-afternoon, and it was dark.

From my rucksack I issued hats, scarves, gloves. Thomas pulled his hat down low and pushed his fingertips through the knit, scratching his scalp. 'Don't say it,' I said. We braced ourselves for the shock of cold, but when the plane door opened, we still bit our lips and nudged ourselves into a huddle in the aisle. I led us out of the plane. The handrail of the steps was etched with frost; the fibres of my woollen gloves stuck to the steel: everything behaves differently in that kind of cold.

My scarf was swathed around my mouth and nose. 'Careful,' I said to the children, but they didn't hear me. Sounds dropped, like in the theatre, as though they were effects: a shout from a ground worker; the ring of metal on metal. I reached the bottom of the steps. There would be ice underneath the snow, and later that night this snow would become ice. I stepped out in my new English boots with solid black soles, listening for the gritty crunch of snow, waiting for my leg muscles to switch on, impulses to fire. I was ready for my limbs, my core, to remember how to walk in snow. But the snow wasn't snow. It was ice, the light of the terminal compacted into each crystal, and it was hard and didn't give, and there was no grip, and I fell.

'Line! Are you hurt?' Arne hitched me under my arm and pulled me up, but I slid again, threatening to bring him down too. 'Hold on to me,' he said, offering me his bulky elbow and grabbing for Thomas with his other hand. 'Thomas – you hold Kristin's hand.'

My trousers were stiffening already with the wet and the cold, and my ankle sang with pain. Each time I placed a foot down, the ground seemed to shift, a minor glacier.

Arne stopped. 'Look at the twins.' All the other passengers had overtaken us; we were the last. The twins were running – *running* – bending, touching the ground, jumping like stars, arms up and out and down, the bobbles on their hats shivering, their gloves swallowing their claps. They didn't put a foot wrong. They could have lived here all their lives.

NORWAY 1962

The Slip

Hilde doesn't feel the pop inside her head, or perhaps it is a tear, but something has changed. She sits with her back against the door to the cupboard in the eaves, the one she has just closed. Her left arm is limp, as though suddenly boneless. Her thoughts bat from one side of her head to the other, but each misses its goal. She cannot remember what she was doing in the cupboard, what she has put in there; she is out of breath and her hands are dusty. The edge of the rug is crumpled; something has been pulled across it. Furniture? A pain in her chest. She knows it: a grief – but now it floats around, unanchored. Why now? She tries to twist, to open the cupboard with her right hand, but she can't shift and she can't reach. The sun sits in the middle of the window at the end of the landing, shining down the hall, honey-warm across her outstretched legs. She tries to remember how she got here.

A walk.
The porch.
A delivery.

That thing – she cannot remember the name for it. Brown, oblong, useful, full. Three initials, but they are swimming around her head.

Her writing, faded, pale, old words. But see – she tries to smile, half smiles – they did their job, those words. They brought the thing home.

Her thoughts skitter away, as if they have fallen off what was barely a path. She watches them tumble, and knows they will always be out of reach.

ENGLAND 1963

What Gets Forgotten

We sold that house with the pear tree in the garden. By then, the tree had stopped producing pears. One summer there were none, then a few the following year, but they had tasted barren. After that, no more.

We returned to that house, just once.

'The pear tree's gone,' I said to my husband, as we stood on the wrong side of the door, before we rang the bell, before we heard footsteps that didn't belong to us. Where the tree had been was now grass, seamless and green.

'Well, you can't blame them,' Arne said. 'A pear tree with no pears.'

I pushed the bell. 'Sometimes they fruit again.'

I had realised the suitcase was missing the night before, when I was on all fours in the eaves of the attic. I tucked the tips of the compacted Christmas tree back into the box and closed the lid, the branches straining against the card as I taped it up. I pushed it into the waiting space, and as I backed out my foot caught a pile of boxes, which collapsed, flushing dust into the air. As I re-stacked them, I lifted their lids and peeked inside: the children's school reports, letters from my mother and Arne's, stained-glass windows made from yellow and orange tissue paper that peeled and flapped away from the black card, the glue now useless. In another box I found our house deeds; we'd untied the pink string and laughed at the old language, the covenants about brewing and pigeons. That was eighteen months ago, a few weeks before my mother's stroke, when her letters stopped, when she forgot how to write, and forgot who we were.

I'd looked around for the suitcase, pebble-brown, with my brother's big initials stamped on the side, the old metal clasps, and leather handles that rattled on brass hinges, a dangling luggage tag that my mother had written out when I left for England. *Why your address?* I'd asked her. *Because the case is mine*, she'd said, angrily. *Your father shouldn't have agreed to you taking it*. When I'd packed, I'd hidden a layer of my brother's belongings under mine. And now, the suitcase was nowhere to be found.

'Hello?' The woman who answered the door wore a pony tail and dungarees. Her lips were chapped, flaking, and her belly was round under the denim. She looked at Arne, and then at me.

'Hello,' I said. 'You bought our house. This one.'

'Oh.' The woman smiled, and I watched her lips to see if they would crack. 'Did we?' Her hand went to her mouth and she picked at a shred of skin. 'Oh, you're the Norwegian couple.'

'I think we left something behind.'

The woman's expression changed, like the tide over sand, and she shook her head. 'I don't think so.'

'Yes, in the loft. A suitcase.'

'No, I'm sure there wasn't anything.'

'Would you mind,' said Arne, 'if we took a look?'

'You can't,' she said. 'It's not a loft any more. It's a bedroom.' She shrugged. 'It might have been thrown away. I could ask my husband if he remembers anything, when he's back?'

I looked at the space where the pear tree had once been, where its untidy branches had spread, its swags of fruit. 'You could have had pears again, you know,' I said to the woman, pointing to the lawn, where the windfalls used to lie. 'If you'd have left it.'

'I'm sorry,' she said, patting a bead of blood on her lip. 'About your suitcase. Was it important?'

NORWAY 1969

Flee, Fly, Flit

Bjørn is to meet me at the station. I didn't want to drive in these conditions, after so many years in England. The last time we saw each other it was summer, and there was swimming and charred fish, and children everywhere. In winter everything is layered – land and people. He stands on the platform, bulky with clothes, and with the years too. His hair is iron-grey, curling out of the bottom of his knitted hat. Mine's still blonde, but a negotiated shade now, and tucked under a hat that feels too much of a statement now I'm here. Bjørn hugs me as though I might sink through the ground at any moment, as though the snow might swallow me. The little sister. But I notice things now, as a stranger would: the stop and start of the snow; the deadening of sound from the sky down; the black, wet, recently spat pellets of chewing tobacco sinking into the drifts as we walk to Bjørn's car in the early afternoon dusk.

'We miss you, Caroline. We have always missed you.' His words are filtered through his scarf, muffled.

Is it worse to be home or away? To miss or be missed? Now I'm here, which has always been home, I'm not sure it *is* home. At this moment I want to run back to Arne in Cambridge, and so surely *home* is the place I want to flee to, not from? *Everywhere is imaginary, if it's not right in front of you.* I'm not sure if I made this up or heard it somewhere, and maybe I don't even agree with it – I think perhaps, if you prod it a little, awful things could lie inside this theory.

'Mother asked for you over and over, before she died.' Bjørn takes his hat off and rests it in his lap. He starts the engine. 'We thought you might come.'

'She had forgotten who I was.'

'She knew.'

'I was planning to come.' I tug on the seatbelt, which jams stubbornly. 'Right after I finished work. I left my job yesterday.' I click the belt and take my hat off, as though I'm apologising for something, and pull off each glove, laying them on my lap. My nails look precious and dainty. 'I had bought plane tickets for the weekend. I was going to surprise you all.'

'Well, she'd have liked that.' Bjørn turns and seems to look straight through me. 'Anything coming?' he asks, nodding towards the road to my right. My window has steamed already and I wipe it with my fist. A vague face reflects back; my hat has flattened my hair, and I shimmy my fingertips through to give it some life.

I look past myself in the car window, down the road. 'I don't think so,' I say, but in fact I can't see much through the steam-streaked, water-beaded glass, through the dark and the fast-falling snow. But in the second before we move, I see eyes, shining and yet black, latching on mine. It must be a deer. Only a deer has eyes that sad.

NORWAY 1969

Funeral

I am bracketed by Arne, in the only suit he owns, and Kristin, tall and beautiful, embarrassed by the balance required between emotion and restraint. A scaffold of air stands between all of us. Thomas is stock-still, not wanting to be obvious. In front of me, small next to Bjørn, my father cries into the crook of his elbow.

People never know what to do with their faces at funerals. It's easier to squeeze a hand than look into a face, where apology sits like lip gloss upon polite smiles. Behind us, row upon row, sits the village. Olav and Wenche and their children, whose names I have forgotten. I try to imagine myself, my life, had I married him, but I cannot unimagine my children, their smells, their demands and expectations and reminders that they are not me. Outside the church, I'd nodded to all those who had stayed when I left, those who never dreamed of leaving. There are old friends I recognise from school days, but their names don't attach to them any more.

On my father's other side is a space on the pew that no one dared to take. It's the size of our eldest brother. The glossy wood of the pew bleeds with stained-glass light; in this fleeting midday window of November daylight the sun has come out, quick as the switch of a light. Our faces are reds and blues and yellows. Then the sun fades again, and the church dims and the colours are fixed back into the windows.

Arne reaches for my hand, as if he knows I'm already wondering how I can bring myself to leave again.

NORWAY 1969

Snow Angel

I sit on the porch, wrapped in one of my mother's quilts. There's a lilting chatter leaking out of the open door behind me, and a chime of crockery as the last of the funeral guests collect dishes, plates, platters. Kristin and Thomas are up in the field behind the house, supervising the building of an army of snowmen. The snow is a novelty for them and they sledge and carve with speed, as though in the morning the white disguise might be gone. They are British in that way. They suffer from doubt – more than I do, more than Arne. 'It's the English weather,' he says. 'The unpredictability. You can't plan; you can never be certain. It affects everything.'

'Lina?' Arne shouts from the kitchen. I draw my feet up onto the wooden seat my father had built and tuck the blanket around my feet.

'Caroline?' This time, my brother Bjørn.

I bend down to look under the bench. My mother's boots are there, as I knew they would be. I pull them on. The wool at the rim has turned slush-grey, and splinters of wood have worked their way in, collected on the patient walks my father used to take her on, through the woods and towards the shore, wading through bracken, the walks she would have forgotten by lunchtime. Her feet had been smaller than mine, and there's a soft pinch at my toes.

'Line!'

I arrange the blanket around my shoulders and jump off the porch into the snow. I walk around the side of the house, and up the hill, each footprint a whisper. I don't slip. In the field I find snowmen but no children. I wander among them, the blanket a cape, its corners dragging in the snow. Some snowmen are taller than me; none of them have faces yet. The field is tangled with tracks and shuffled footprints. I head further up the field where the snow is virgin. I toss the blanket onto the fence and hitch my black dress up.

NORWAY 1969

Meditation

The fjord looks like a lake some days. It would be easy to believe in a final shoreline, just out of sight. My father and I had set off at ten; he set the pace, and now we stand on one of the hills behind the village. The surface of the water blinds us occasionally with a midday glim.

'You have your mother's boots on.'

'Yes.'

'Do they fit?'

'They're comfortable.'

My father is still catching his breath from the uphill walk, and his words tumble out upon the crest of an exhale. I breathe in time with him, like I used to do with the twins. It's not the end of the world, I used to tell them. Breathe. I do it quietly so he doesn't notice. I breathe in time with the mild waves that will be washing the posts of the jetty below us, like I breathed with the waves of pain in labour. I breathe in time with the idle beat of the wings of a soaring bird above us, like I breathed the first night I was a wife. I breathe in time, just in time, to stop all the memories coming at once.

The air is icy on my cheeks; it pinches my lungs. 'What if I came back, Dad? What if we all came back?'

My father puts his arms around me and holds me as if I am seven again. I don't pull away from the scratch of his beard.

'Line, I'm going.'

I step back and almost slip on hidden ice. 'What do you mean?'

'I'm leaving the village. I'm going to live in the city.' He sighs, clouding the air. 'I would have gone years ago but your mother wouldn't leave. Every reason I had to go, she had a reason to stay.' He smiles at me, his eyes watering at the corners. 'It was often the same reason.'

I usher the snow into a small pile with the toe of my mother's boot, pushing and nudging and tapping.

My father watches me. 'Bjørn and Elin and the children will move into the house. Bjørn is a good teacher. He needs to stay. He belongs here.' He takes his hat off and strokes his glove across the thin, pink skin of his head. 'I will live in an apartment.'

'But it rains more in the city,' I say.

'Yes.' My father pulls his scarf up over his mouth. 'Isn't it great?' His eyes sparkle and he turns away from the view. 'I love the rain.'

NORWAY 1970

Father and Son

'Caroline doesn't like my apartment.'

'She doesn't think you should have moved.'

'It's not that. I mean, you're right. But that's not why she doesn't like it.'

'It's none of her business, Dad.'

'I know.'

'You like it, don't you?'

'I do. I feel . . . like an animal there. An underground one. Like I can hide away and only come out if I want to. When I want to.'

'Like a burrow.'

'Yes. I suppose. Will you be happy, Bjørn, all of you, living in the house?'

'We will. The house is ready for a new start.'

'You should paint it. Change it from the outside at least.'

'Perhaps.'

'I think blue would be nice. Get rid of the red. I can help, in the spring.'

'With your hip? They'll always call it Henrik's place, or Hilde's place, you know.'

'Well, at least you won't forget us. Anyway, they won't always. Things move on. You should paint the bedroom. Paint it white. Stop it smelling of the woods.'

'It doesn't smell of the woods, Dad. That's in your head.'

'No wood in my new apartment, did you notice? Stone. Inside and out.'

'I hadn't noticed, no.'

'Do you remember how your mother used to grow strawberries? No one else's grew, but hers did.'

'I remember, Dad.'

'Your mother said it was because of the bees. No bees, no strawberries.'

'Caroline used to put honey out to feed the bees. When they got tired.'

'Really, Bjørn? Huh. I never knew that.'

'They looked like they were dead, but she never believed they were. She left teaspoons of honey water next to them.'

'Did it work?'

'Most of the time. Sometimes they *were* dead, and I had to move them.'

'Maybe they were just taking longer to revive.'

'Yes, Dad. Maybe.'

'What time is Caroline coming?'

'She'll be with us by evening.'

'Let's buy some honey. We can have it with bread. Toast my new home.'

NORWAY 1970

A New Home

Caroline waves to her father and Bjørn. She will join them later at her father's new apartment. It sits on the ground floor of a cobbled street, with other buildings pressing upon it from either side. When she stands in it, she feels surrounded, from above, from the edges, but perhaps that is what her father wants, after all.

He hasn't taken much with him – mostly small things, clearing surfaces, ready for Bjørn and his family. Bjørn's wife was happy to keep most of the furniture, as if evicting large pieces might weaken the structure of the house.

Caroline's memories are shared between both houses: the one she lived in until she was fifteen and the one that was rebuilt in its place. The foundations are the same; the layout is the same, and the dimensions too. But it is a different house. She supposes the first house was the ghost, but it's the new one that has always seemed unreal, fragile. It smells different; the air is thinner; the joints creak differently. When she dreams, it is of her first bedroom, the first house.

She climbs the stairs and passes her old/new room. The door is ajar and she clicks it closed, as she has done to the rest of the doors in the house, as though to trap the whispers. Her room will soon belong to Bjørn's son, her brother's surprise – and adored – third child. She passes, too, the room that had never belonged to Espen but that still had to be built, had to fill the space left between the other rooms, the room that had no function but to remind them that he never lived in this new version of their home. That door was always closed. The sun glints, now, through the gable-end window, casting a whiskey-yellow square on the door that leads to the cupboard in the eaves. She reaches for the handle, in case her father has forgotten anything in this out-of-the-way space.

She slides out a large basket and lifts the lid Christmas decorations: stars and burnished fruit, silver candle holders and half-wilted candles. She opens the cupboard door fully and the sun spills into the space. Behind the box, she sees it. The brown suitcase, leather handles, her brother's initials, the label dangling, with this address, her mother's writing. The suitcase Caroline last saw in the attic of the house with the pear tree that had forgotten how to fruit.

ENGLAND 1970

Leave/Live

'Look what I found when I was helping Dad move,' I say, as I throw open my red suitcase on our double bed. Inside is another suitcase, nesting. Arne looks at me, deep query lines on his forehead.

I run my hands over the hard shell. 'My suitcase. Well, Espen's suitcase.'

'The one we lost?'

'The one we left behind in the old house. Yes.'

'You found it in Norway?'

I lift the old case out and place it on the bed next to the red one. 'It was in my parents' house, hidden away in a cupboard.'

'How the hell did it get there?'

I shrug and tug the label off. The old card frays into fibres where it has ripped. I hand it to Arne. 'See. My parents' address was on it all this time. Maybe someone returned it. The man who bought our house. One of their builders.' I grin. 'We'll never know. I don't care.'

Arne looks into my own half-empty case. 'Where are the rest of your clothes?'

'I left them behind. I'll pick them up next time we visit.'

'It's strange,' says Arne, 'that your mother never mentioned the case had been returned.'

'I suppose.'

'Are Espen's things still inside?'

'Yes.' I bend down and push the suitcase into the dark, grey space under our bed. 'His watch. Photographs. Things he collected.'

'You're going to keep it under the bed?'

'Is that all right?'

Arne closes my red suitcase and clicks the latches. 'I'll put this away for you.' I watch him climb onto the stool and heft the case into the built-in cupboard. He's heavier than he used to be, but he is also even gentler. His hair is longer than it's ever been, curling on his neck, tufting above his ears. His jumper lifts up as he reaches, the skin on his torso still pale and young. He pushes the cupboard door, and it shuts with a suck-kiss of the magnet clasp. He leaps down, and the room shakes. He launches onto our bed, pulling me with him.

'Did we make all the right choices?' I ask, propped onto my elbows, as though I'm fifteen again.

Arne looks at the ceiling. 'We take decisions, we make the story. We never have the full picture, so the outcome is part luck, part fate, part evidence.'

'*Those* don't sound like the words of a scientist.'

Arne widens his eyes in mock outrage. 'Lots of luck in science. Lots of chance.' He pokes me on my arm. 'Took a chance on you, didn't I? Big risk.'

I poke him back, between two ribs, where he's ticklish. 'That's not science, idiot. That's love.'

'Chemistry, then.' He laughs.

I lean my head on his chest and close my eyes, feel the swell and release of his lungs.

'I've got a surprise,' he says into my ear. 'Kristin and Thomas will be home soon. The four of us are going out for dinner to celebrate your new job.'

'That'll be nice. I can't believe I start tomorrow. It'll be good to work again.'

'You'll be the best museum guide they've ever had. You were never meant to sit behind a desk.'

'Where are we going? For dinner?'

'The new Italian place in the village.'

'Nice.'

'How was your dad's new apartment?'

I open my eyes. 'Actually, when I went back I liked it. It suits him. He made the right choice.'

'I missed you,' says Arne. 'I'm glad you're home.'

'I'm glad too,' I say, and I think I mean it.

Acknowledgements

Endless thanks to the Bath Novella-in-Flash Award team, for running the brilliant competition that led to this novella, and to publisher Ad Hoc Fiction. It's been a real honour to work with Jude and John, and to contribute to their championing of flash fiction. Barrels of appreciation also go to the competition's judge, author Michael Loveday, who has provided invaluable feedback and made careful and nuanced editorial suggestions prior to publication, all of which have improved the final text no end.

Some of these chapters were written during a Meg Pokrass workshop, chapters that helped give the story its final shape. Thank you to Meg and the participants for prompts, comments and feedback.

I'm also immensely grateful to Jane Hammett for her excellent proofreading input, particularly the curbing of commas! Thanks also to my lovely friend Emma Shakoor for allowing me to use one of her beautiful paintings for the cover.

I'd never have kept writing without strict instructions to do so from my course tutor Sarah Schofield in 2016. I'm so glad I did as I was told.

Finally, thanks to my family for leaving me to it and cheering me on in equal measure.

Previously Published

Grateful acknowledgement to the editors of the following publications, where earlier versions of these chapters previously appeared:

'Learning to Share' (2018) *Ellipsis Zine* [Online] Available: http://www.ellipsiszine.com/learning-to-share-by-johanna-robinson/

'Heartwood' (2019) Reflex Fiction [Online] Available: https://www.reflexfiction.com/heartwood-flash-fiction-by-johanna-robinson/ [Print] (2019) in *The Real Jazz Baby: Reflex Fiction Volume Two*, Reflex Fiction

About the Author

Originally from the northwest of England, Johanna has also spent time in Leeds, Bradford, Oslo and Sydney. In 2011 she returned to Liverpool, where she lives with her family and works as a freelance proofreader, via an English degree and law. Johanna wrote her first short fiction in 2016 on the Liverpool Comma Press short story course, and her work has since appeared in *Strix*, *Ellipsis Zine*, the Brighton Prize anthology and *Reflex Fiction Volume Two*. She was shortlisted for the Dinesh Allirajah Prize 2019 and has been longlisted for a number of other prizes. Her interest in the WWII Norwegian resistance began in 1996/97 when she spent a year at Oslo University on the Erasmus exchange scheme. More writing information can be found at www.johanna-robinson.com.

About the Artist

Emma Shakoor grew up on the coast and most of her paintings are inspired by the sea. Her earlier works feature textured choppy seas and dark stormy skies. Currently she is painting much gentler paintings. They depict softer, smooth beachscapes and horizons, with a strong focus on the beautiful light at the beach. The painting Johanna chose for her novella cover is called *Beach Huts*. Emma lives in Yorkshire with her husband and two daughters.